Why Does Need a Wagon?

Dr. Blake Brandes
Valerie Brender
Lola Svetlova

MotivationalMillennial

Dragon returns
To his hometown of Sprout
Carrying a gift
For Pig in his mouth.

He lands next to Pig
Who is fixing his bike.
"I brought you a bell
That I thought you might like."

"Thank you," says Pig.
"It's always a pleasure
When you return home
Bringing me treasures."

"You're welcome," says Dragon.
"Can I show you a trick—
Something I learned
While out on my trip?"

"Pig, look here
At what I can do!
I can breathe fire
And fly right through!"

He looks back at Pig
With a grin on his face,
Approaching a tree
At a perilous pace.

"Watch out!" cries Pig
As Dragon flies through the ring.
The thwack of a limb!
The crack of a wing!

Pig rushes over
To check on his friend.
He looks at the wing,
"This will take time to
mend."

Dragon asks Pig,
"Oh what will I do?
I can't fly home.
It hurts me to move."

Dragon lives in the mountain
Next to the town.
It's a long way up
And a long way down.

Pig says to Snake,
"I've got an idea.
Will a log work?
I've got one right here!"

That's a great start,
But if we fumble,
The log will slip,
And Dragon will tumble!

Pig looks around
And finds some rope.
"Could we use this
To get up the slope?"

"Ouch!" says Dragon.
"The ground will be bumpy.
By the time I get home,
I might be grumpy."

Dragon looks sad,
"What if nothing will work?
What if I stay stuck,
Hurt in the dirt?"

"We'll figure this out.
We can't give up!
Let's think some more…
We'll get unstuck."

Snake searches the town
All over the ground
And suddenly shouts,
"Look what I found!"

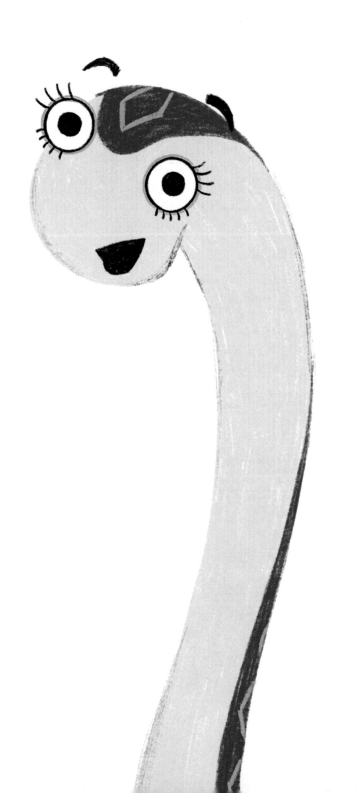

There it was,
Bright and blue,
An empty wagon.
"Now this will do!"

They push and they pull!
They lift and they heave!
And finally Dragon
Is ready to leave.

Snake takes the handle.
Pig takes the rear.
The wagon starts rolling...
They let out a cheer!

They huff and they puff.
They grunt and they sweat.
"We can make it," says Pig.
"We're just not there YET!"

At last they arrive.
They knock on the door.
At first no one answers,
So they knock some more.

The door flies open.
It's Mama Dragon.
She gasps as she sees
Her son in a wagon.

"I learned a new trick
And tried it in town.
But I messed it up
And crashed to the ground."

"That happens sometimes
When we try something new.
We'll fix up your wing
And try for Round Two!"

In the weeks that follow,
They wheel Dragon to school,
To the park, to the movies,
The store, and the pool.

One day Dragon finds
That he can flap again.
He takes to the skies.
He flies in the wind.

His friends gather round.
Mama Dragon arrives,
"Are you ready to try
Your trick one more time?"

He watches for branches.
He looks out for trees.
He waits until there's
No wind and no breeze.

Then Dragon breathes fire
Into a ring.
He soars right through...
Nothing touches his wing!

His friends all cheer.
He takes a bow.
"I couldn't do it at first,
But I can do it now!"

ISBN 978-1-7373128-0-2

First edition August 2021

MotivationalMillennial

Motivational Millennial
2721 Shattuck Avenue 1001
Berkeley, California 94705
BlakeBrandes.com